DRONE BALONEY

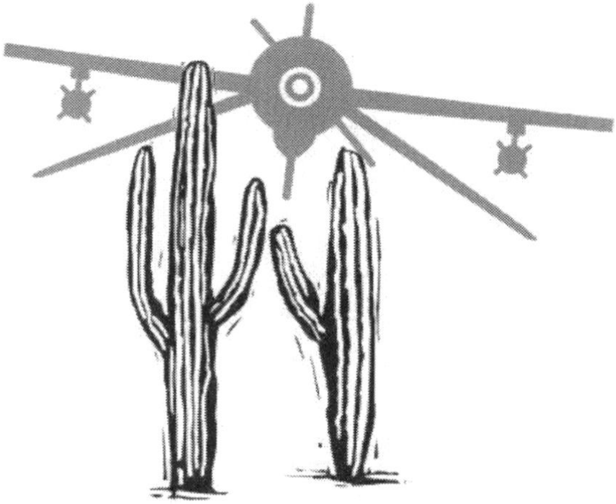

A Novel
By
John Hewitt

John Hewitt's other novels in the Baja Trilogy

Under the Padre's Thumb

Stranger in Baja